Classics for Beginning Readers

Reader's Digest Young Families

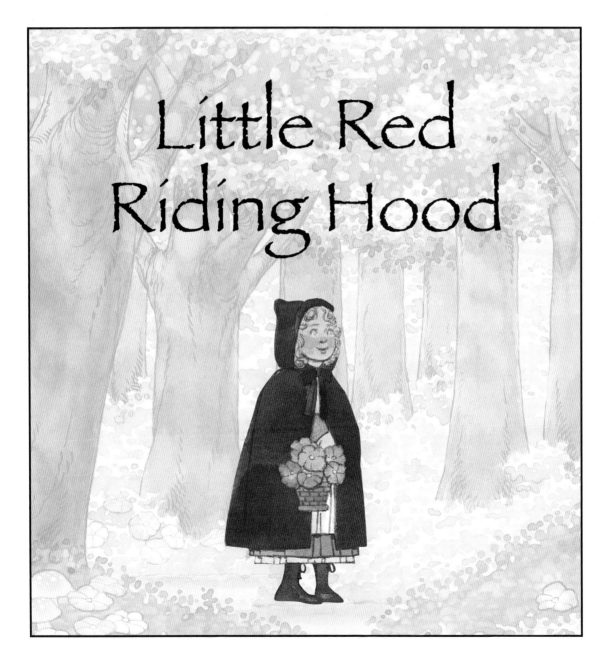

Little Red Riding Hood

Designers: Elaine Lopez and Wendy Boccuzzi
Associate Editorial Director: Pamela Pia

Adapted text by Suzanne Gaffney Beason copyright © 2003 Reader's Digest Young Families, Inc.
Based on the original story written by Charles Perrault.
Illustrations by Walter Velez ©2003 Reader's Digest Young Families, Inc.

The Classics for Beginning Readers logo and Reader's Digest Young Families
are registered trademarks of The Reader's Digest Association, Inc.

ISBN-10: 1-59939-098-1   ISBN-13: 978-1-59939-098-7

Printed in China.

Reader's Digest Young Families

Little Red Riding Hood

Based on the story written in 1697
by
Charles Perrault

Retold by Suzanne Gaffney Beason

Illustrations by
Walter Velez

$\mathcal{O}$nce upon a time there was a sweet little girl who was loved by her mother, grandmother, and everyone else. But her grandmother doted on her most of all and made her a little red hood and cape. Everywhere she went, she was called Little Red Riding Hood.

One day Little Red Riding Hood's mother said to her, "Your grandmother is not feeling well. Would you please bring her these breads I have baked and this little dish of butter?"

Since Little Red Riding Hood often dawdled, her mother warned her to go straight to her grandmother's house without stopping along the way. The girl happily set off on her journey to the next village.

As Little Red Riding Hood strolled through the woods, she met a wolf. He would have very much liked to eat her right then and there, but he dared not because some woodcutters were working nearby in the forest.

The wicked wolf asked the little girl where she was going. "I am going to see my grandmother," she answered, not knowing that it was dangerous to speak to a wolf.

"Does your grandmother live far away?" asked the wolf.

"Oh, yes," replied Little Red Riding Hood. "She lives beyond this forest in the next village. Her house is the first one you come to."

"Well now," said the clever and cunning old wolf, "I think I shall go and see your grandmother, too. I will go by this path, and you by that path, and we will see who gets there first.

The wolf set off running with all his might by the shorter road, and the little girl continued on her merry way by the longer road.

As Little Red Riding Hood wandered down the path, she amused herself by gathering nuts, chasing after butterflies, and making bouquets of wildflowers.

The wolf quickly arrived at the grandmother's house. He knocked on the old woman's door.

Knock, knock.

"Who is there?" asked the grandmother.

"It is your granddaughter, Little Red Riding Hood," said the wolf, disguising his voice. "I've come to see how you are. I've brought you some bread and a little dish of butter from my mother."

"How wonderful," said the grandmother, who was resting in bed. "Lift the latch and open the door."

The wolf did just as the old woman had instructed. He lifted the latch and the door flew open.

As soon as the wolf entered, the grandmother could see that this was not her precious Little Red Riding Hood. When she realized it was a wolf, she fainted with fright.

The wolf quickly picked up the old woman and put her in a nearby cupboard.

Next, the clever wolf put on one of the grandmother's nightgowns and caps to disguise himself. He crawled into the bed and waited for Little Red Riding Hood to arrive.

At last, there came a knock at the door.
"Who is there?" asked the wolf, knowing very
well it was Little Red Riding Hood.

When Little Red Riding Hood heard the wolf's gruff voice, she was startled. But thinking that her grandmother had a bad cold, she replied, "It is your granddaughter, Little Red Riding Hood. I've brought you some bread and a little dish of butter from my mother."

"Put the bread and the little dish of butter on the chair," said the wolf, "and come sit up on the bed with me."

Little Red Riding Hood did as she was told and placed the bread and the little dish of butter on the chair. Then she took off her beautiful red cape.

As Little Red Riding Hood came toward her grandmother's old feather bed, the wolf pulled the covers up tightly under his chin. When Little Red Riding Hood climbed onto the bed, she was amazed by her grandmother's appearance.

"Oh, Grandmother!" Little Red Riding Hood exclaimed, "what big arms you have!"

"All the better to hug you with, my dear!" said the wolf.

"Oh, but Grandmother, what big ears you have!"

"All the better to hear you with, my dear!"

"And Grandmother," Little Red Riding Hood continued, "what big eyes you have!"

"All the better to see you with, my dear!"

"But Grandmother, what big teeth you have!"

"All the better to EAT you with, my dear!"

Then the wolf threw back the covers and leaped out of bed. He was just about to gobble up Little Red Riding Hood when his big feet got tangled up in the lace bedspread. The wolf tripped and fell to the floor. Little Red Riding Hood escaped through the door.

Inside the cupboard, the grandmother awoke with a start. She sprang from the cupboard and grabbed a broom in one hand and a skillet in the other. Then she chased the wolf out the door. He was never seen again!

After she was certain that her grandmother was fine, Little Red Riding Hood ran all the way home. She didn't stop once to gather nuts or chase butterflies or pick flowers. And she didn't stop to talk to even one wolf. For you see, Little Red Riding Hood had learned this very important lesson:

> *Little ones, this seems to say,*
> *Never stop upon your way.*
> *As you're witty, so be wise;*
> *Wolves may lurk in every guise.*
> *Now as then, 'tis simple truth—*
> *Sweetest tongue has sharpest tooth!*